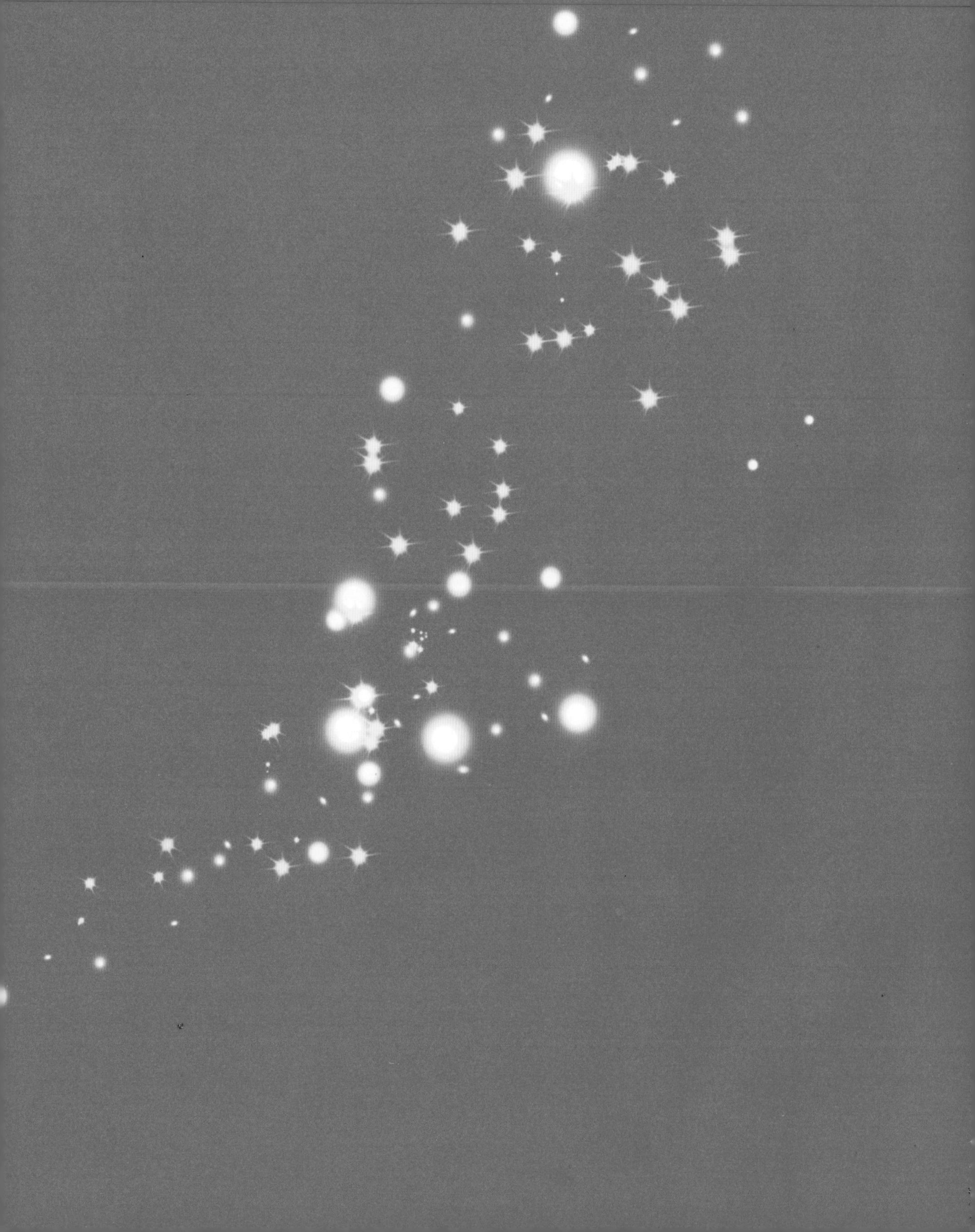

SYBIL
the Backpack Fairy

1
"NINA"

MICHEL RODRIGUE • Writer
ANTONELLO DALENA & MANUELA RAZZI • Artists
CECILIA GIUMENTO • Colorist

PAPERCUTZ™
New York

To my mother, Giuseppina
– MANUELA RAZZI

To my father
– ANTONELLO DALENA

Thanks to Manuela
and Antonello for their trust.
Thanks to Stéphanie for her help
and to Hélène for the "pandigole."
To Kalixte and Pascale my backpack fairies!
– MICHEL RODRIGUE

Sybil the Backpack Fairy
#1 "Nina"
MICHEL RODRIGUE – Writer
ANTONELLO DALENA & MANUELA RAZZI – Artists
CECILIA GIUMENTO – Colorist
JOE JOHNSON – Translation
JANICE CHIANG – Lettering
Production by SHELLY STERNER, Nelson Design Group, LLC
Associate Editor – MICHAEL PETRANEK
JIM SALICRUP
Editor-in-Chief

ISBN: 978-1-59707-285-4

Printed in China
November 2011 by PWGS
Block 623 Aljunied Road #07-03B
Aljunied Industrial Complex 389835

Distributed by Macmillan.

First Papercutz Printing

DRRRING

YOUR TURN TO PLAY! HEY DON'T SHAKE 'EM SO MUCH!

GOTTA DO WHATCHAGOTTA DO...

OWW!

OUCH!

HEY, THERE'RE ONLY TWO DICE! WHERE'S THE THIRD ONE?

I WARNED YOU...

YOU SHOOK TOO HARD! NOW IT'S SICK...

YEAH? WHO'S THIS?

MASCAREIGNE! A THROW FOR NOTHING!

‹BLUURK!›

YEAH... WHO'S THAT?... I'LL GET HIM FOR YOU.

‹BLAHHHH!›

GIMME THAT. I'M GONNA CLEAN 'EM!

NO? OH! IS THAT RIGHT? NO KIDDING? AT LAST! WE'RE GOING!

AND WHEN DO WE LEAVE? RIGHT AWAY? BUT—

WHAT ABOUT MY GAME OF GROANING DICE? YEAH... OKAY, 'COMING...

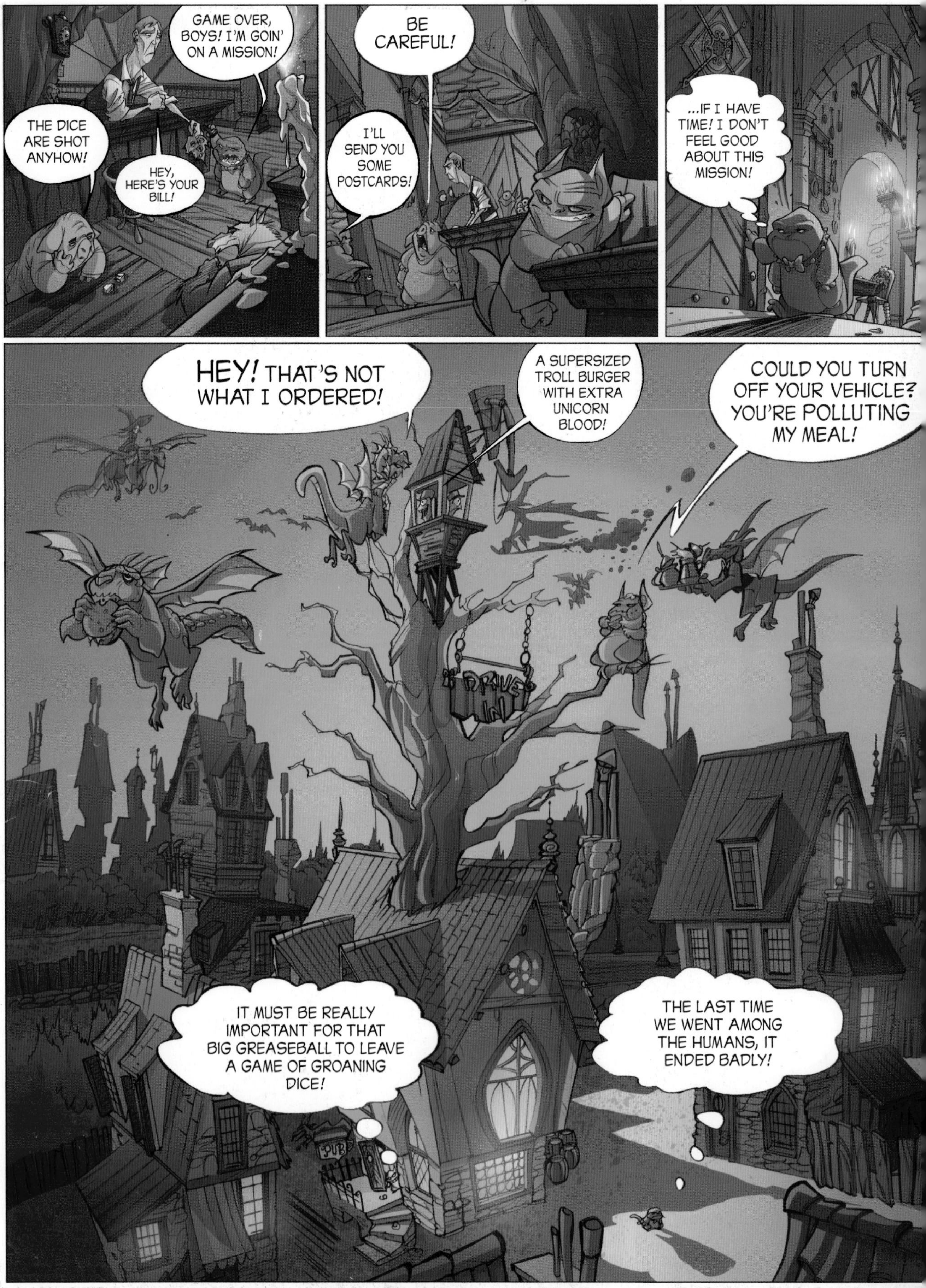
GAME OVER, BOYS! I'M GOIN' ON A MISSION!
THE DICE ARE SHOT ANYHOW!
HEY, HERE'S YOUR BILL!
BE CAREFUL!
I'LL SEND YOU SOME POSTCARDS!
...IF I HAVE TIME! I DON'T FEEL GOOD ABOUT THIS MISSION!
HEY! THAT'S NOT WHAT I ORDERED!
A SUPERSIZED TROLL BURGER WITH EXTRA UNICORN BLOOD!
COULD YOU TURN OFF YOUR VEHICLE? YOU'RE POLLUTING MY MEAL!
DRIVE IN
IT MUST BE REALLY IMPORTANT FOR THAT BIG GREASEBALL TO LEAVE A GAME OF GROANING DICE!
THE LAST TIME WE WENT AMONG THE HUMANS, IT ENDED BADLY!
PUB

NINA! GET A MOVE ON! WE'RE ALREADY LATE!

YEAH, YEAH. WHATEV...

MEEOOOW!

YOU CHANGE YOUR TONE WITH ME! AND I'VE ALREADY TOLD YOU I DON'T WANT TO SEE THAT CAT ON THE TABLE! IT'S NOT SANITARY!

KEEKAT!

NINA, HURRY UP! I'VE GOT TO DROP YOUR BROTHER OFF AT THE NEW BABYSITTER'S BEFORE TAKING YOU TO SCHOOL! AND I HAVE AN IMPORTANT MEETING TODAY!

OKAY, MOM! OKAY!

COME ON! INTO THE CAR! TAKE YOUR BACKPACK!

UH... WHERE'S MY BAG?

WHAT DO YOU MEAN "WHERE IS IT"? YOU DIDN'T GET IT READY LAST NIGHT?

WELL, YES, I DID! I SET IT RIGHT HERE!

NINA! PLEASE DON'T TELL ME YOU'VE LOST YOUR BACKPACK ON THE FIRST DAY BACK TO SCHOOL...?

BUT, MOM I SWEAR! I LEFT IT RIGHT HERE!

KEEKAT! MAMA!

OKAY, MOM, OKAY!

YOU'VE GOT 30 SECONDS TO FIND YOUR BAG AND GET IN THE CAR. AFTER THAT, IT WON'T BE MY PROBLEM!

I ALREADY HAVE MY KEYS!

I'M TELLING YOU-- I'LL TAKE YOU TO SCHOOL WITHOUT YOUR BACKPACK! YOU'LL SORT IT OUT WITH YOUR TEACHER!

AND DON'T COUNT ON ME WRITING HER AN EXCUSE FOR YOU!

HERRR! HERRR!

NINA! THERE'S YOUR BACKPACK! ON THE SWING-SET!

WHAT? WHERE?

ALL RIGHT! I'M LATE!

'COMING, MOM!

I SWEAR TO YOU-- I DON'T UNDERSTAND HOW--

LATER! WE'LL TALK ABOUT IT TONIGHT! EVERY TIME YOU GET BACK FROM SUMMER VACATION, YOU'RE IMPOSSIBLE!

NOT ONLY DO YOU RUN LATE ON THE FIRST DAY BACK, BUT YOU MAKE ME LATE, TOO!

HUWW! HUWW! KEEKAT!

IT'S NOT FAIR! IT'S NOT FAIR! I'M TIRED OF IT!

GO ON, SEE YOU TONIGHT! KISSES, IN ANY CASE!

KISSES! SEE YOU TONIGHT, MOM!

OKAY! LET'S THINK!

MOM'S CONVINCED I'M LYING TO HER, AND—

HEY!

OH, IS THE TOMBOY STILL ASLEEP?

LAURIE! DON'T YOU START AGAIN OR I'LL—

WHOA! THE LITTLE MISS IS GETTING MORE AND MORE GIRLY!

LEAVE HER ALONE, LAURIE!

LET IT GO, NINA! SHE'S JUST TRYING TO GET YOU KICKED OUT!

YEAH, SHE'S JEALOUS OF YOU!

WELL, THERE'S NO REASON TO BE!

DRIIING

SOMETHING REALLY WEIRD HAPPENED TO ME THIS MORNING! I'LL TELL YOU ABOUT IT DURING THE BREAK.

OKAY, THEN, IT'S NOT THE CAT, NOT THE BABY! WHO THEN? AND— AND WHAT IF IT WAS ME?

WHAT IF I'M SLEEP-WALKING? MAYBE IT'S SOMETHING REALLY SERIOUS!

NINA! COULD YOU REPEAT WHAT I JUST SAID?

UH— WELL...

WELL... I... THE... THE...

?

...THE UNITED STATES OF AMERICA HAS A POPULATION OF 300 MILLION INHABITANTS!

...THE UNITED STATES OF AMERIC... HAS A POPULATION OF 300 MILLION INHABITANTS!

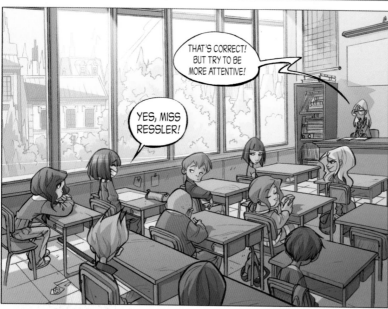

THAT'S CORRECT! BUT TRY TO BE MORE ATTENTIVE!

YES, MISS RESSLER!

LAURIE! HOW MANY INHABITANTS IN CHINA?

1.3 BILLION, MISS RESSLER! BUT THE POPULATION'S STARTING TO STAGNATE AND SHOULDN'T KEEP ON GROWING SO FAST!

THANKS, JENNA!

I DIDN'T DREAM THAT! SOMEONE WHISPERED THE ANSWER TO ME! AND JENNA DOESN'T LIE TO ME! IT WASN'T THAT BIG IDIOT, AND IT CAME FROM THE LEFT!

TAKE OUT YOUR NOTEBOOKS AND WRITE...!

BUT I DIDN'T SAY ANYTHING TO YOU!

HUH?

WHAT IF I'M CRAZY?! CRAZY AND A SLEEPWALKER?!

EEEK!

WHO JUST SHRIEKED?

NINA! ON THE FIRST DAY OF THE SCHOOL YEAR, I'M ASKING YOU TO BE A LITTLE MORE ON YOUR GAME! THAT'S MY ONE AND ONLY WARNING! GOT IT?

BUT— ÷SIGH!÷ YES, MISS RESSLER!

FLAP

FLAP

AAAH!

IIEE!

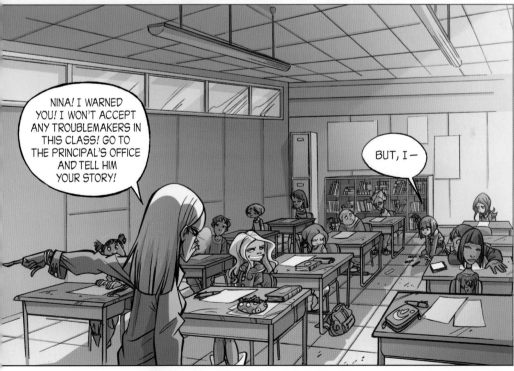

NINA! I WARNED YOU! I WON'T ACCEPT ANY TROUBLEMAKERS IN THIS CLASS! GO TO THE PRINCIPAL'S OFFICE AND TELL HIM YOUR STORY!

BUT, I—

WHAT WAS THAT THING? A MOUSE? ARE MICE LIVING IN MY BACKPACK? ARE THEY THE ONES THAT PUT IT ON THE SWING? CAN MICE EVEN DO THAT?

SO, WHAT DID HE SAY TO YOU?

ARE YOU OKAY, NINA?

HE REALLY GOT ON MY CASE AND GAVE ME SOME LINES TO COPY FOR TOMORROW! IT'S REALLY NOT MY DAY!

⸮HEEE! HEEE!⸮

AND THAT WITCH OVER THERE! I'M GOING TO—

NO! YOU'D GET ALL THE BLAME. SHE'D LOVE THAT!

SO, WHY DID YOU SCREAM LIKE THAT?

THERE WAS A MOUSE IN MY PENCIL CASE!

A MOUSE?

LOOK! THE PROOF! IT EVEN ATE MY COOKIES! I'VE GOT NOTHING LEFT TO SNACK ON!

!⸮!

!⸮!

HERE, HAVE THIS! I LOST MY APPETITE!

I'M SICK OF IT! IT'S BEEN NON-STOP SINCE THIS MORNING! I FIND MY BAG OUTSIDE, THERE ARE MICE IN IT, AND I'M THE ONE PUNISHED!

YOU KNOW, NINA, YOU MUST BE STRESSED OUT! YOUR PARENTS GOT SEPARATED DURING SUMMER VACATION. MAYBE YOU'RE DISTRACTED!

YEAH— I DON'T KNOW!

YOU'D BETTER GET IT TOGETHER! WE HAVE A MATH QUIZ NOW!

OH, JOY! MATH! GREAT! I'M SURE HAVING A GOOD TIME TODAY!

AAH!

HELLO, NINA! YOU'RE EVEN CUTER THAN IN THE PHOTOS!

DON'T BE AFRAID! I'M HERE TO HELP YOU! HAVE NO FEAR!

WHO ARE YOU? WHERE DO YOU GET OFF LIVING IN MY BACKPACK? WHERE ARE YOU FROM? WHAT ARE YOU DOING IN THERE?

NINA!

I ASKED FOR QUIET DURING THE ASSIGNMENT! EVERYTHING MUST BE DONE IN TEN MINUTES!

YES, MISS RESSLER.

IT'S ALL YOUR FAULT! THAT MAKES TWO TIMES THAT I GOT CAUGHT!

WHAT A MESS! AND I DON'T UNDERSTAND ANYTHING ABOUT THIS MATH!

I'M GONNA GET ANOTHER BAD GRADE! IT'S A DISASTER! A TOTAL DISASTER!

OH, NO! DON'T GET UPSET! I TOLD YOU I WAS HERE TO HELP YOU! WATCH AND LET ME DO IT.

WHOA! COOL!

AND THERE! THIS QUIZ WAS EASY!

SWEET! AND IT'S EVEN IN MY HANDWRITING!

NINA!

NINA! I'VE HAD IT! I'M CALLING YOUR MOM IN FOR A CONFERENC TOMORROW

ON THE FIRST DAY OF THE SCHOOL YEAR, YOU GET LINES TO COPY AND A PARENT-TEACHER CONFERENCE FOR ME! GOOD JOB, LITTLE LADY! AND WHAT EXPLANATION DO YOU HAVE FOR YOURSELF?

WELL— UH— IF I TELL YOU, YOU'LL NEVER BELIEVE ME!

THE PENCIL BAG MOVED ON MY DESK, AND A MONSTER WAS STUCK TO MY PENCIL! AND THE FAIRY DID THE MATH WORK FOR ME, AND—

AND—

WAIT! I'M GOING TO SHOW HER TO YOU! SHE'S REALLY CUTE, AND THE MONSTER'S SUPER FUNNY!

NINA, NINA...

INA! INA!

IF THIS KEEPS ON, I'M GOING TO TAKE YOU TO SEE A COUNSELOR! SO, STOP YOUR LYING AND YOUR FOOLISHNESS RIGHT THIS MINUTE! I HAVE TO GO OUT TONIGHT, AND YOU'RE BABYSITTING YOUR BROTHER! BUT NO TV, CANDY, OR CAKES! UNDERSTOOD?

WHAT--?

UNDERSTOOD, LITTLE LADY?

YES, MOM! AND WHERE ARE YOU GOING? ARE YOU COMING HOME LATE?

RICHARD'S TAKING ME TO DINNER! CALL ME ON MY CELL PHONE IF YOU NEED ANYTHING AT ALL!

⇝SIGH!⇜ RICHARD! HE'S STUPID AND UGLY! HE'S AN IDIOT!

DING DONG

NINA, PLEASE! RICHARD'S A VERY NICE GUY AND— THAT MUST BE HIM! GO LET HIM IN!

NOW THIS! THE IDIOT'S HERE. WILL THIS DAY EVER END?!

HELLO, MISSIE. HOW'S IT GOING?

HELLO, ID— UH— RICHARD!

OKAY! I'M READY! SEE YOU SOON, SWEETIE!

MMM— HAVE A NICE EVENING, MOM!

WHO'S THE HUNK? I DON'T HAVE HIM IN MY FILES!

AN IDIOT! OF NO INTEREST!

I DON'T UNDERSTAND A THING! I TOLD THE TRUTH, AND MOM DOESN'T BELIEVE ME! IT'S ALL CRAZY! BAH! HEY, WANT TO SEE A MAGIC TRICK!

INA! INA!

ABRA-KADABRA! TA-DAH!

YUMM! YUMM!

HEY LOOK! CANDY!

BUT— WHERE DID YOU GO?

WE WERE THERE! IN YOUR BACKPACK!

⇝SLURP!⇜

RIGHT! SO, NOW CAN YOU TELL ME WHO THE TWO OF YOU ARE?

DON'T WORRY, NINA! WE'RE HERE FOR YOUR OWN GOOD! TO HELP YOU!

TO HELP ME?! HELP ME GET IN TROUBLE...?

OF COURSE NOT! I'M SYBIL, AND HE'S PANDIGOLE. HE'S MY PERSONAL ASSISTANT. HE'S NOT MEAN, BUT HE DOES HAVE A WICKED SWEET TOOTH!

I CAN DO YOUR HOMEWORK, YOUR LINES TO COPY, AND ANY OTHER CHORES! YOU JUST HAVE TO GIVE ME SOMETHING TO EAT!

BUT THEN— THIS AFTERNOON, MY SNACK! YOU'RE THE ONE WHO ATE IT!

ME, A LITTLE... PANDIGOLE, A LOT! I'M WATCHING MY FIGURE!

WE THOUGHT IT WAS FOR US...! OH! ONE TINY, IMPORTANT DETAIL: NEVER SAY "THANK YOU" TO ME! IT OFFENDS ME... AND THEN I DISAPPEAR!

BUT, IF YOU'RE SEEN? YOU RISK—

THERE'S NO RISK! ONLY YOU OR AN ANIMAL CAN SEE US!

SERIOUSLY... ARE YOU A REAL FAIRY?

AS REAL AS THEY COME! HERE, WATCH!

MEEOWWW!

I CAN DO FUN THINGS LIKE THIS!

OR LIKE THAT!

AWESOME!

CONVINCED THEN, MISS NINA?

WHOA! THAT'S COOL!

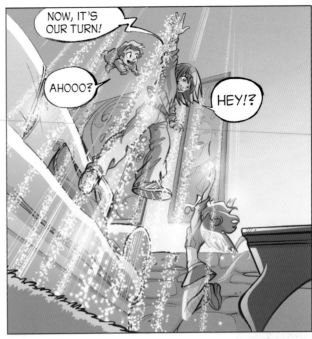

NOW, IT'S OUR TURN!

AHOOO?

HEY!?

MOLDY MOZZARELLA! THIS TRICK OF YOURS IS COOL!

MREOWW!

COO! COO!

HEEHEEHEE!

MRAOW! MEOW!

OH, NO! NONE OF THAT, YOU FAT KITTY!

THERE WE GO! BREAK'S OVER! EVERYBODY COME BACK DOWN!

THAT WAS SO COOL! WE'LL DO IT AGAIN, OKAY?

WE'LL SEE, WE'LL SEE...!

COO! COO!

MY CANDY!

‹BURRP!›

WELL, HE'S NOT VERY NICE! HOW SELFISH!

I TOLD YOU SO: HE'S A GLUTTON! DON'T YOU HAVE ANY HOMEWORK FOR TOMORROW?

YES! WHAT A PAIN! THE LINES, PLUS A REPORT ON RAMSES II!

HMM, THE LINES WILL BE KNOCKED OUT QUICKLY!

TEEP! TEEP! TEEP! THE LINES ARE DONE! TEEP! TEEP! TEEP! LET'S CELEBRATE!

I CAN GET USED TO THIS, SYBIL!

LIKE THIS! LOOK!

SO, YOU WERE SAYING— A REPORT ON RAMSES II! THAT'S NOT VERY DIFFICULT! WOULD YOU LIKE TO MEET THE REAL RAMSES II?

HOW?

HELLO TO YOU, SYBIL! IT'S BEEN AGES SINCE YOU LAST VISITED MY COURT.

HELLO TO YOU, GREAT KING! I PRESENT TO YOU... NINA!

I MUST BE DREAMING...!

YOU KNOW EACH OTHER?

OH, FOR CENTURIES NOW!

YOU MUSTN'T EXAGGERATE! I'M NOT AS OLD AS ALL THAT!

THIS'S EXCELLENT! IT'S WAY BETTER THAN ON TV!

NOTE WELL THE DIFFERENCES IN CLOTHES AND JEWELS!

I'D LIKE TO GO WITH THEM!

OH, NO! WE CAN TALK TO THEM, BUT THEY CAN'T COME OUT OF THAT BUBBLE! IT WOULD BE CATASTROPHIC!

TOO BAD! HEY!

BAD CAT! COME BACK HERE!

¡HRRRRG!¡

GIVE PANDIGOLE BACK TO US! HE'S NO GOOD FOR YOU!

HE'S GOING TO REGRET HIS MISTAKE!

OOH! CALM DOWN! YES, MY BEAUTIES, YOU NEED TO STRETCH YOUR LEGS!

LET'S GO GALLOP A LITTLE!

YAAAA!

WHAT'S THAT?

RAMSES II! DIDN'T YOU EVER GO TO SCHOOL?

AND DON'T YOU EVEN THINK OF TRYING THAT AGAIN!

I THINK HE'S LEARNED HIS LESSON!

MEEOWR!

OOPS!

?!?

I DID SOMETHING TOTALLY STUPID! BY GOING AWAY, I WAS NO LONGER CONTROLLING THE BUBBLE! BUT WHERE'S RAMSES?

OH... MY--! IT'S A DISASTER!

THAT WAY! LOOK! THE DOOR!

OH, NO! HE WENT OUT! WE HAVE TO GO GET HIM BACK BEFORE HE CAUSES A DISASTER!

BUT I CAN'T LEAVE LEO HERE ALL ALONE! AND THE OTHERS?

YEAH--

CARRY YOUR BROTHER ON YOUR BACK! AS FOR THEM, WITHOUT THEIR KING, THEY WON'T BUDGE FROM HERE! LET'S GO!

I HOPE YOU KNOW WHAT YOU'RE DOING. I'LL CLOSE THE DOOR, JUST IN CASE...

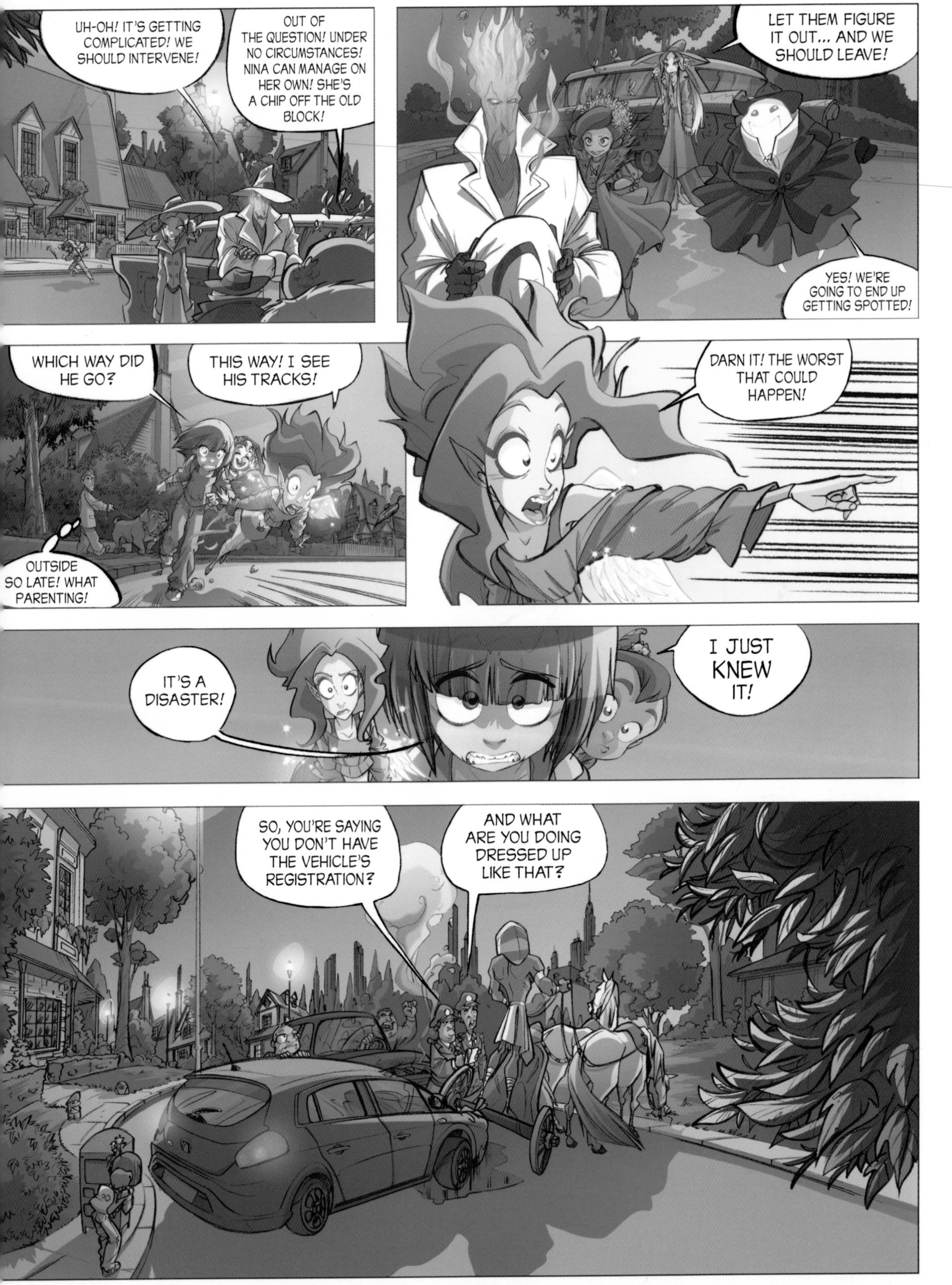
UH-OH! IT'S GETTING COMPLICATED! WE SHOULD INTERVENE!
OUT OF THE QUESTION! UNDER NO CIRCUMSTANCES! NINA CAN MANAGE ON HER OWN! SHE'S A CHIP OFF THE OLD BLOCK!
LET THEM FIGURE IT OUT... AND WE SHOULD LEAVE!
YES! WE'RE GOING TO END UP GETTING SPOTTED!
WHICH WAY DID HE GO?
THIS WAY! I SEE HIS TRACKS!
OUTSIDE SO LATE! WHAT PARENTING!
DARN IT! THE WORST THAT COULD HAPPEN!
IT'S A DISASTER!
I JUST KNEW IT!
SO, YOU'RE SAYING YOU DON'T HAVE THE VEHICLE'S REGISTRATION?
AND WHAT ARE YOU DOING DRESSED UP LIKE THAT?

NOT TALKING? THEN YOU'RE COMING WITH US TO THE POLICE STATION!

ANOTHER DRUG ADDICT! I'M SURE OF IT!

SPEAK WITH DEFERENCE TO THE KING OF KINGS! MISERABLE WORMS!

SNAP

SNAP

OUCH!

OWW!

QUICK, NINA! IT'S NOW OR NEVER!

HEY! MY FRIENDS! WHAT A NICE SURPRISE!

SPEAKING OF SURPRISES...!

WE MUST LEAVE QUICKLY, GREAT KING!

EVERYTHING'S ALL RIGHT! DON'T WORRY! IT'S FOR A MOVIE!

AH! OKAY! I THOUGHT SO, TOO...

LET'S RETURN TO THE HOUSE, GREAT KING!

AT YOUR ORDERS, MY FAIRY!

REGARDLESS, THOSE MOVIE PEOPLE ARE REALLY GOOD! DID YOU BELIEVE THAT?

WELL... I HOPE THEY HAVE GOOD INSURANCE!

YAHH!

FASTER! FASTER! NINA'S MOTHER WILL SOON BE HOME!

HEY! WATCH WHERE YOU'RE GOING, YOU PACK OF 🌟✨⭐

LOOK AT THOSE CRAZY KIDS! THEY'LL DO ANYTHING TO SET THEMSELVES APART!

BE CAREFUL! HE'S ZIG-ZAGGING!

DADA! DADA!

IF MOM SAW US, SHE'D FREAK OUT!

MOM?!

NINA?! BUT--? BUT--?!

MOMMY! MOMMY!

RICHARD... THERE... NINA... THE—!

THE CHARIOT? YES, WELL, WHAT ABOUT IT?

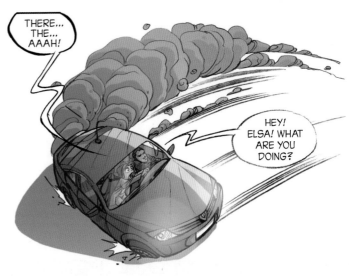

THERE... THE... AAAH!

HEY! ELSA! WHAT ARE YOU DOING?

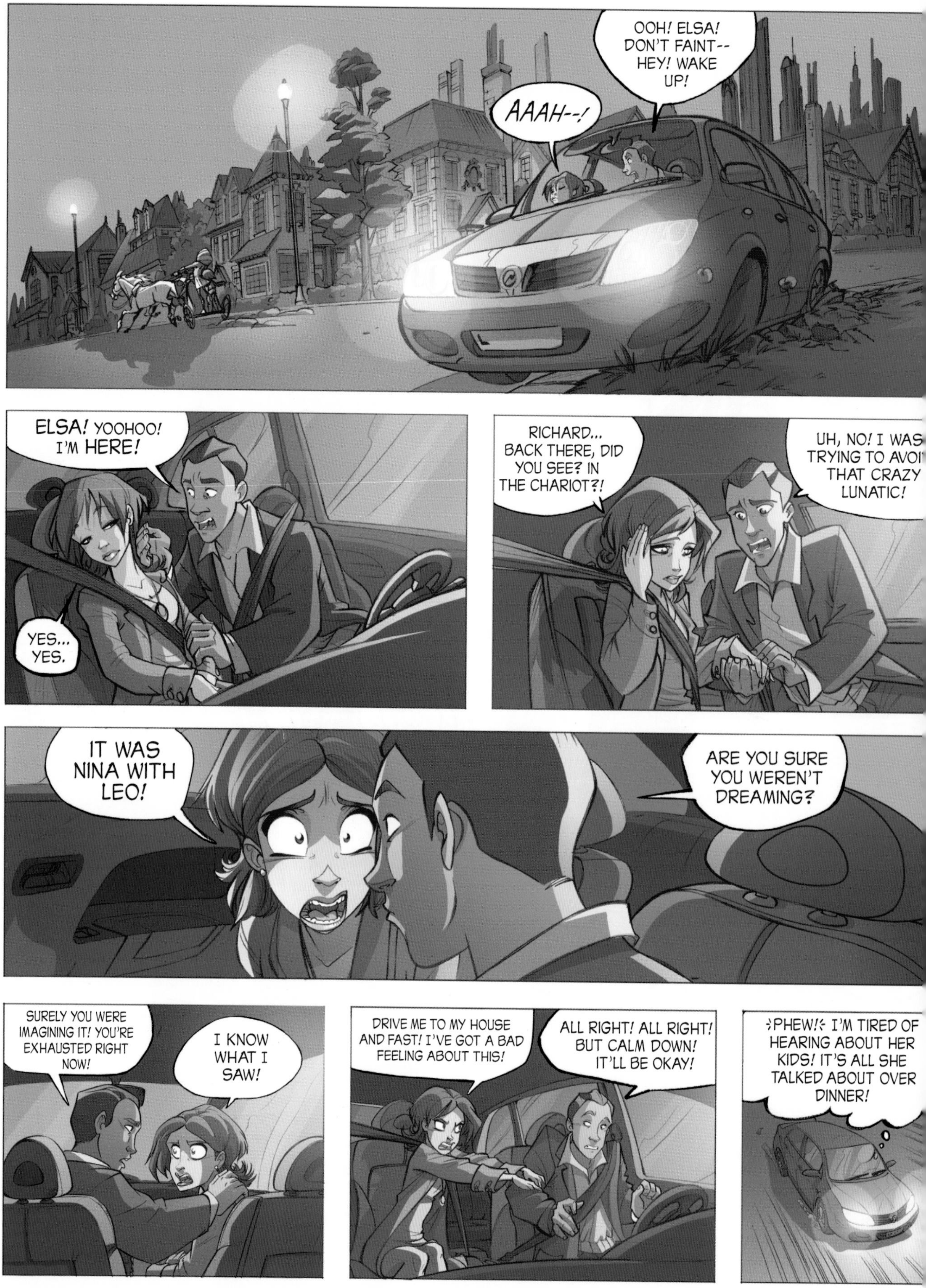
OOH! ELSA! DON'T FAINT-- HEY! WAKE UP!
AAAH--!
ELSA! YOOHOO! I'M HERE!
YES... YES.
RICHARD... BACK THERE, DID YOU SEE? IN THE CHARIOT?!
UH, NO! I WAS TRYING TO AVOI THAT CRAZY LUNATIC!
IT WAS NINA WITH LEO!
ARE YOU SURE YOU WEREN'T DREAMING?
SURELY YOU WERE IMAGINING IT! YOU'RE EXHAUSTED RIGHT NOW!
I KNOW WHAT I SAW!
DRIVE ME TO MY HOUSE AND FAST! I'VE GOT A BAD FEELING ABOUT THIS!
ALL RIGHT! ALL RIGHT! BUT CALM DOWN! IT'LL BE OKAY!
PHEW! I'M TIRED OF HEARING ABOUT HER KIDS! IT'S ALL SHE TALKED ABOUT OVER DINNER!

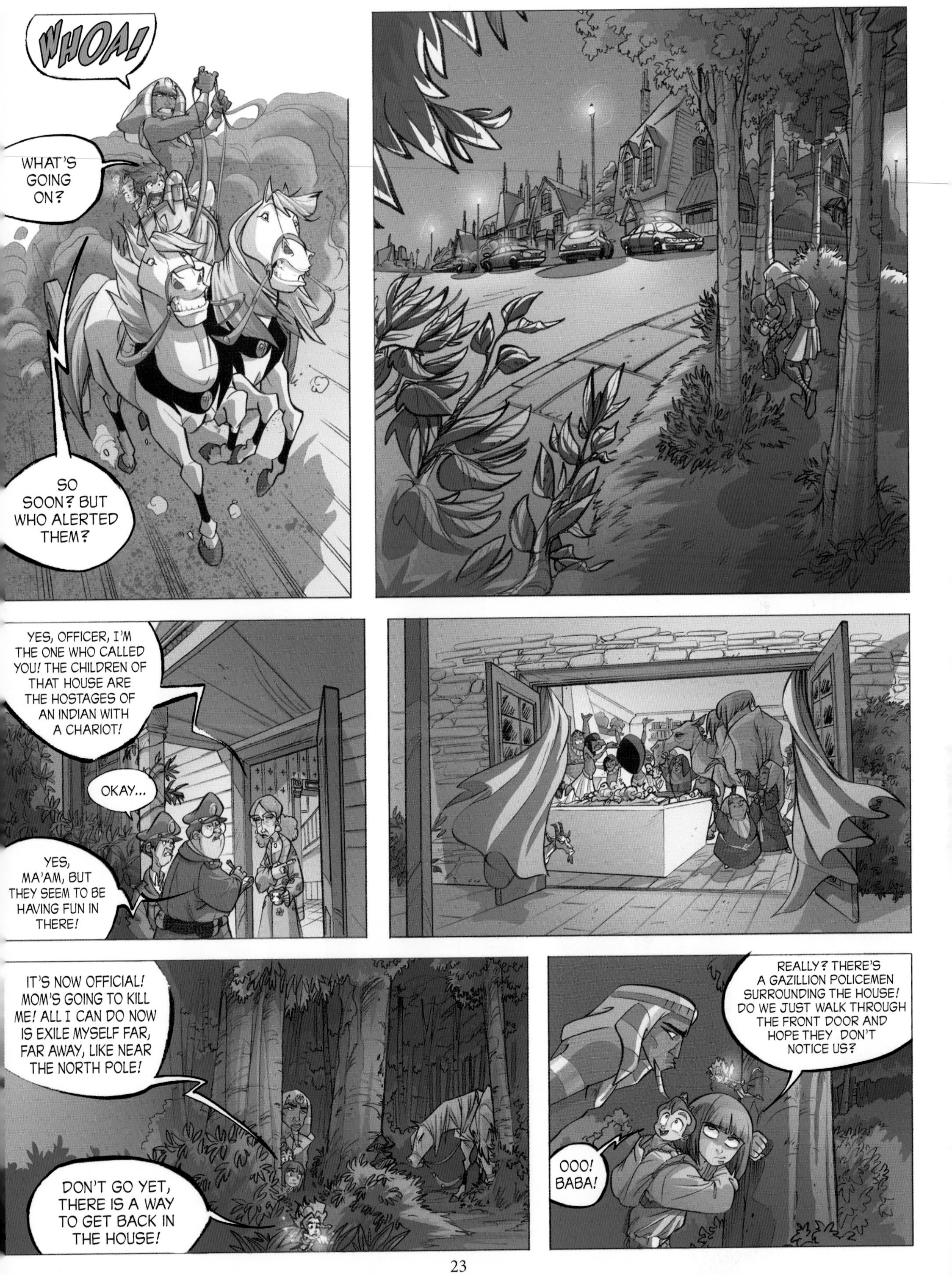
WHOA!
WHAT'S GOING ON?
SO SOON? BUT WHO ALERTED THEM?
YES, OFFICER, I'M THE ONE WHO CALLED YOU! THE CHILDREN OF THAT HOUSE ARE THE HOSTAGES OF AN INDIAN WITH A CHARIOT!
OKAY...
YES, MA'AM, BUT THEY SEEM TO BE HAVING FUN IN THERE!
IT'S NOW OFFICIAL! MOM'S GOING TO KILL ME! ALL I CAN DO NOW IS EXILE MYSELF FAR, FAR AWAY, LIKE NEAR THE NORTH POLE!
DON'T GO YET, THERE IS A WAY TO GET BACK IN THE HOUSE!
REALLY? THERE'S A GAZILLION POLICEMEN SURROUNDING THE HOUSE! DO WE JUST WALK THROUGH THE FRONT DOOR AND HOPE THEY DON'T NOTICE US?
OOO! BABA!

LET'S NOT BE SO NEGATIVE, NINA! SUCH AN ATTITUDE RARELY HELPS! THERE'S AN ENTRANCE YOU DON'T YET KNOW ABOUT! FOLLOW ME!

IT'S HERE UNDER THE GAZEBO! I DIDN'T WANT TO SHOW IT TO YOU YET...!

JUST NEED TO SAY A FEW MAGIC WORDS...

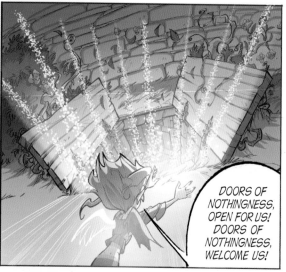

DOORS OF NOTHINGNESS, OPEN FOR US! DOORS OF NOTHINGNESS, WELCOME US!

GO IN! GO IN, MY LITTLE RABBITS! THAT GAZEBO WILL BE YOUR TOMB!

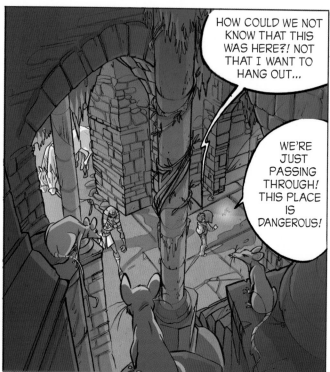

HOW COULD WE NOT KNOW THAT THIS WAS HERE?! NOT THAT I WANT TO HANG OUT...

WE'RE JUST PASSING THROUGH! THIS PLACE IS DANGEROUS!

END OF THE LINE, SYBIL! YOU AND YOUR LITTLE PROTÉGÉS WON'T BE GOING ANY FARTHER!

AMANITE!

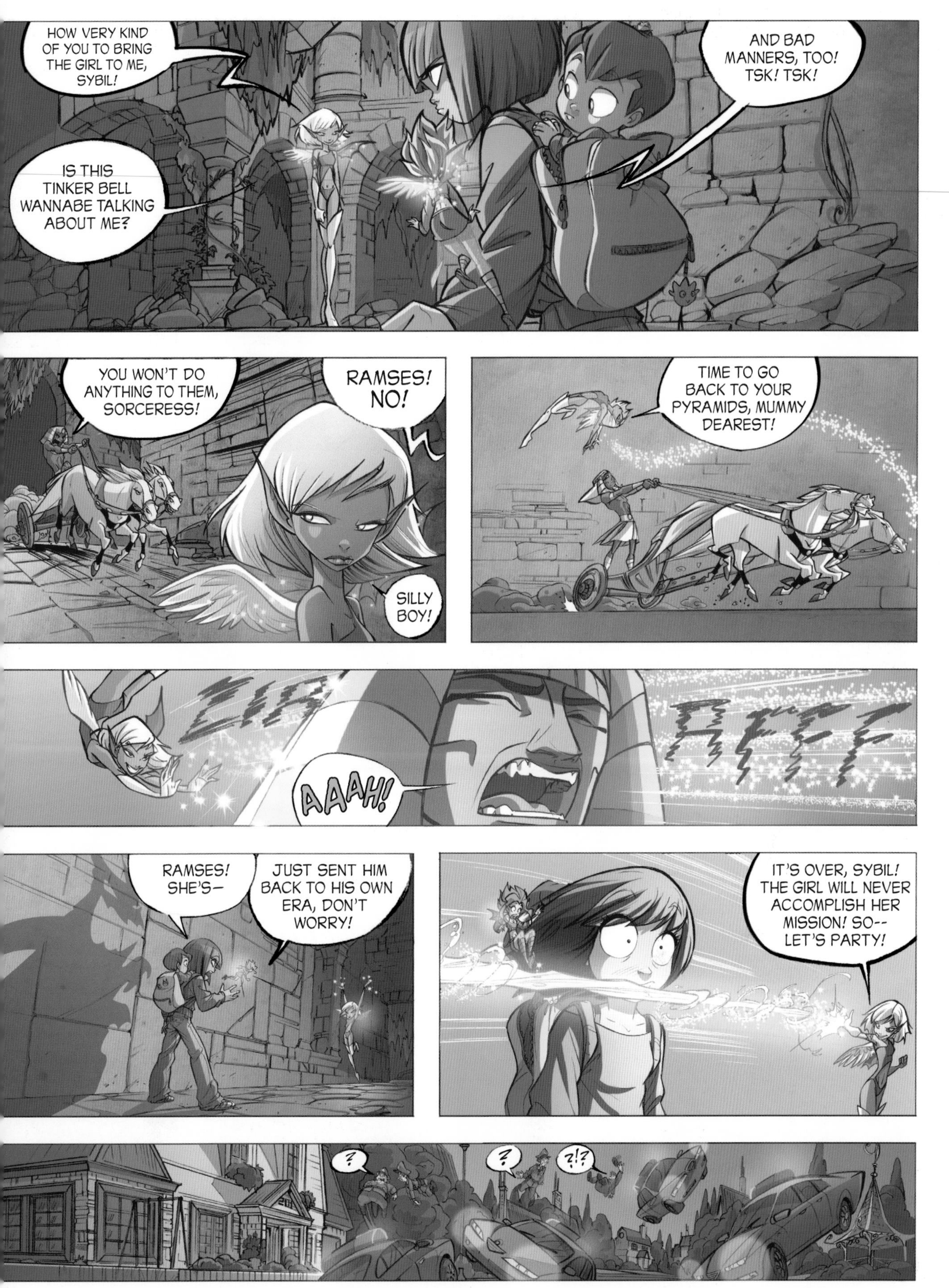
HOW VERY KIND OF YOU TO BRING THE GIRL TO ME, SYBIL!
IS THIS TINKER BELL WANNABE TALKING ABOUT ME?
AND BAD MANNERS, TOO! TSK! TSK!
YOU WON'T DO ANYTHING TO THEM, SORCERESS!
RAMSES! NO!
SILLY BOY!
TIME TO GO BACK TO YOUR PYRAMIDS, MUMMY DEAREST!
ZIB
AAAH!
RFFF
RAMSES! SHE'S—
JUST SENT HIM BACK TO HIS OWN ERA, DON'T WORRY!
IT'S OVER, SYBIL! THE GIRL WILL NEVER ACCOMPLISH HER MISSION! SO-- LET'S PARTY!
?
?
?!?

PAARRRRTTYY!

SAY HI TO CRASHER! HE'S QUITE THE PARTY ANIMAL— HERE TO CELEBRATE YOUR FAILURE!

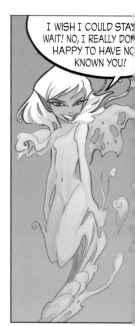

I WISH I COULD STA... WAIT! NO, I REALLY DON... HAPPY TO HAVE NO... KNOWN YOU!

PAARRRTTTYY!

NINA! WATCH OUT!

BBRRRAAMM

THAT WAS REALLY UNCALLED FOR, BIG BOY!

ARE YOU OKAY, LEO?

ABOOM! ABOOM!

PAARRTTYY!

BRAH-KOOM

HEY! HE'S NOT VERY NICE!

HI-YAH!

WAK

:SNORT!:

THIS ISN'T LOOKING GOOD FOR US...!

ABOOM! ABOOM!

MOM WON'T EVER BELIEVE ANY OF THIS!

ARRGH

YO, "TONS OF FUN," LOOK AT ME!

PARTY'S OVER! IT'S BEEN A REAL BLAST!

PAARR--

RRRRARAM

-TEEEEEE··

WHERE DID HE GO?

WE'RE IN NO MORE DANGER! I SENT HIM BACK WHERE HE CAME FROM!

INDEED!

MY GAME!

I WAS WINNING!

ME, TOO!

UH... PARTY?

OWW! OUCH!

...LET'S SEE, A SHELF, A PITCHER OF BRUTAL, SIX BOTTLES, ONE DART BOARD...

I'LL ADMIT DOING HOMEWORK WITH YOU ISN'T AT ALL BORING, IT'S EXCITING!

THAT MAY'VE BEEN TOO EXCITING! LET'S GET BACK ON TRACK, AND PICK UP WHERE WE LEFT OFF...

BABOOM! ABOOM! ♪HEEHEEHEE!♪

THAT'S RIGHT! WITH ALL THAT DRAMA, I ALMOST FORGOT ABOUT MOM!

HURRY UP, NINA!

OOH!

DID YOU SEE ALL THAT, SYBIL? HOW DID YOU KNOW ABOUT THIS PLACE?

QUESTIONS LATER! SAVE YOUR BREATH FOR RUNNING!

COME ON! JUST A LITTLE MORE, WE'RE ALMOST THERE!

INSIDE THE HOUSE?

UHM.. NOT EXACTLY!

THE HOUSE IS SURROUNDED! RELEASE THE CHILDREN!

WHAT?! WE'RE IN A BASEMENT?

YOUR HOUSE IS BUILT ON TOP OF THE RUINS OF AN OLD MANOR! THE BASEMENT IS ALL THAT IS STILL LEFT!

WE MADE IT! WE'RE HOME!

WE STILL MUST BE CAUTIOUS— WE'RE NOT OUT OF DANGER YET...

AND WHO WAS THAT--?!?

OH, NO!

JUST LOOK AT THE MESS THEY'VE MADE OF EVERYTHING! IT'S A DISASTER!

DON'T PANIC! I CAN FIX THIS!

GIVE YOURSELVES UP! RELEASE THE HOSTAGES!

30

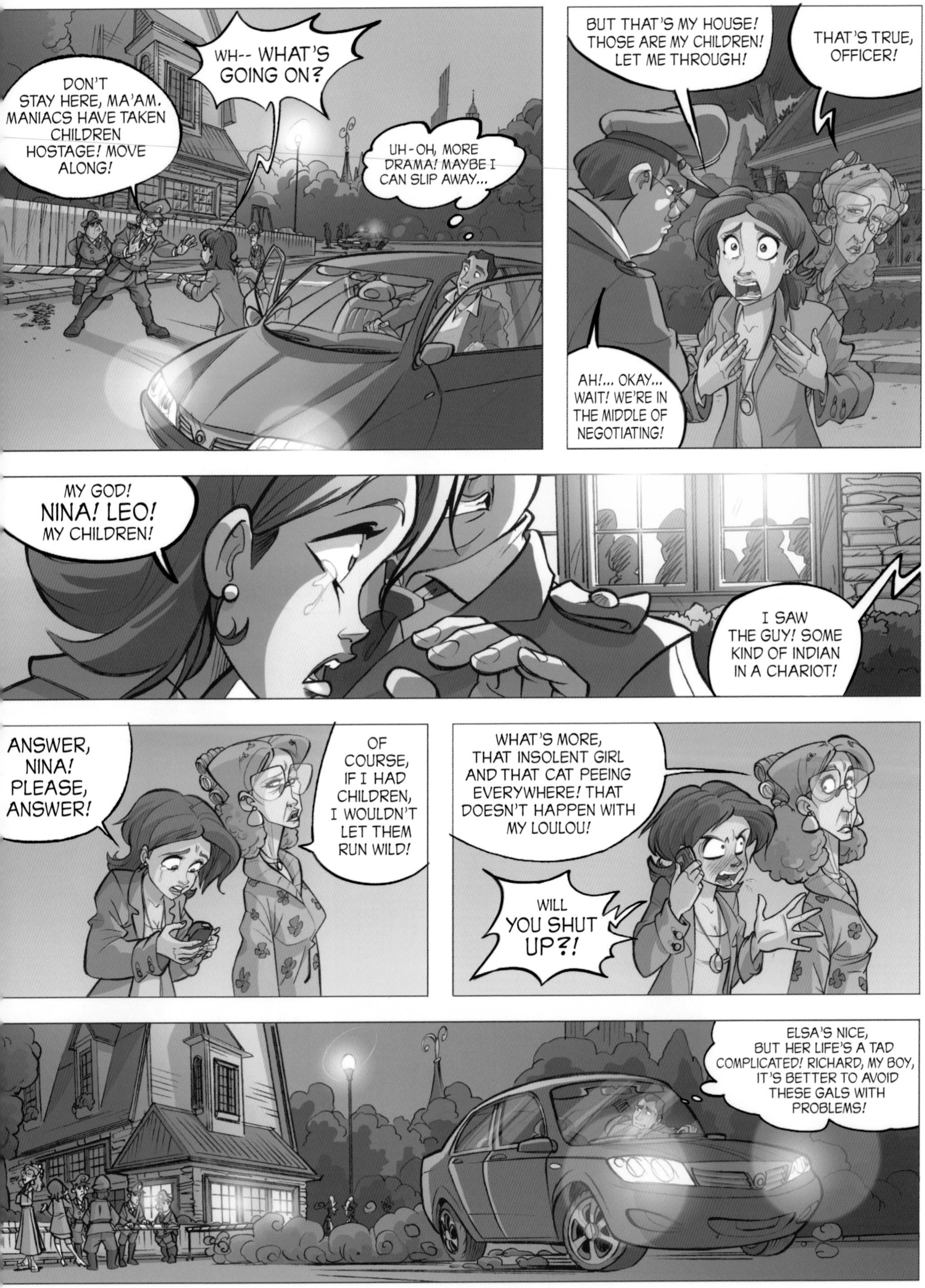
WH-- WHAT'S GOING ON?
DON'T STAY HERE, MA'AM. MANIACS HAVE TAKEN CHILDREN HOSTAGE! MOVE ALONG!
UH-OH, MORE DRAMA! MAYBE I CAN SLIP AWAY...
BUT THAT'S MY HOUSE! THOSE ARE MY CHILDREN! LET ME THROUGH!
THAT'S TRUE, OFFICER!
AH!... OKAY... WAIT! WE'RE IN THE MIDDLE OF NEGOTIATING!
MY GOD! NINA! LEO! MY CHILDREN!
I SAW THE GUY! SOME KIND OF INDIAN IN A CHARIOT!
ANSWER, NINA! PLEASE, ANSWER!
OF COURSE, IF I HAD CHILDREN, I WOULDN'T LET THEM RUN WILD!
WHAT'S MORE, THAT INSOLENT GIRL AND THAT CAT PEEING EVERYWHERE! THAT DOESN'T HAPPEN WITH MY LOULOU!
WILL YOU SHUT UP?!
ELSA'S NICE, BUT HER LIFE'S A TAD COMPLICATED! RICHARD, MY BOY, IT'S BETTER TO AVOID THESE GALS WITH PROBLEMS!

HELLO— NI... NINA?

AND RUDE TOO! THAT'S SINGLE WOMEN FOR YOU!

YES! IT'S ME, MOM!

EVERYTHING'S OKAY, MOM! NO! NO! THERE'S NO HOSTAGE-TAKING! THE ONLY STUFF HAPPENING IS ACTUALLY KIND OF FUNNY...

THESE ANIMALS CAME INTO THE HOUSE AND THEY'VE MADE A BIG MESS! NO! NO! LEO AND I ARE FINE! YOU CAN COME IN!

DID YOU SAY... ANIMALS?

OH! MY POOR BABY! I WAS SO SCARED! I EVEN THOUGHT I SAW YOU IN A CHARIOT ON THE ROAD! WHERE DID ALL THESE ANIMALS COME FROM?

I'M THINKING THE CIRCUS IS IN TOWN...

WE'LL HAUL THESE ANIMALS TO THE CITY ZOO!

THANK YOU, OFFICER!

WELL! YOU CERTAINLY HAD QUITE A NIGHT!

WAS YOUR DINNER NICE?

YOU KNOW... WITH ALL THIS EXCITEMENT I COMPLETELY FORGOT ABOUT RICHARD!

IT'S NO BIG DEAL, HE'S AN ID— U GOODNIGHT MOM!

FEELING BETTER, MOM? YOU'RE NOT UPSET WITH ME, ARE YOU?

NO, SWEETIE! BUT IT'S TIME TO GO TO SLEEP! DON'T FORGET THAT THERE'S SCHOOL TOMORROW!

AND TOMORROW, I'LL ALSO HAVE TO CLEAN THIS ALL UP! OH, WELL! IT'S NOT EVERYDAY I HAVE A CAMEL AND GOATS IN MY LIVING ROOM!

IT'S LESS BORING THAN GOLDFISH!

OR A CAT!

EEEK!

MY POOR MACAROON! MAYBE NINA REALLY DOES NEED A CHILD-PSYCHOLOGIST...

...OR PERHAPS I SHOULD PAY MORE ATTENTION TO HER!

TELL ME, SYBIL...

SURE YOU SENT THE EGYPTIANS BACK TO THEIR TIME, BUT I HAD TO LIE TO MY MOM! AND THOSE POOR ANIMALS...!

WE HAD NO CHOICE, NINA! AND THE SOLUTION FOR THE ANIMALS WAS BRILLIANT!

THEY'LL BE TREATED WELL AT THE ZOO! AND YOU CAME OUT OF THAT JUST FINE!

BUT WHO IS THAT AMANITE? AND WHAT'S THAT MISSION SHE WAS TALKING ABOUT? WHAT'S ALL THAT ABOUT? YOU'RE HIDING THINGS FROM ME!

WE'LL TALK ABOUT IT SOON ENOUGH! TRUST ME! ANYWAY, I'M PROUD OF YOU! HEY, PANDIGOLE, COVER YOUR MOUTH WHEN YOU YAWN!

⨠YAAWWNN!⨠ I CAN'T! I'M HOLDING THE MIRROR!

YOU'RE RIGHT! IT WAS A REALLY COOL EVENING! WE HAD AN AWESOME TIME! SLEEP WELL, SYBIL! GOODNIGHT, PANDIGOLE!

SLEEP TIGHT, NINA! TILL TOMORROW!

GOOD-- ⨠ZZZ!⨠

I CAN'T **BELIEVE** EVERYTHING THAT HAPPENED TO ME TODAY! I HAVE A NEW FRIEND ALL TO MYSELF! AND SHE'S A FAIRY, TOO! AND PANDIGOLE IS... FUNNY!

⨠RRONK⨠ ⨠WHEEZE⨠ ZZZ!

WHAT'S MORE, HE SNORES!

YOU'VE FAILED, AMANITE! THAT'S NOT GOOD!

I'VE NOT BEEN WORKING ON MY GRAND PLAN FOR CENTURIES FOR EVERYTHING TO FALL APART BECAUSE OF SOME GIRL AND SOME NOBODY FAIRY! SO, ACT QUICKLY AND FIX THIS USING ANY MEANS NECESSARY! OTHERWISE, I'LL CUT "YOUR" LOSSES!

⸬GULP!⸬

LIKE THIS!

H! THAT'S MEAN! T'S GONNA TAKE DAYS FOR IT TO STICK BACK ON! AND WHERE'S MY WIG?

BUT I'M GOING TO BE MAGNANIMOUS! TO HELP YOU IN YOUR TASK, I'M SENDING YOU A SPECIAL ALLY!

LOOK! IT'S A CHARMING YOUNG GIRL FULL OF JEALOUSY AND SPITE.

GREAT! WHAT'S HER NAME?

LAURIE! ISN'T SHE CUTE?

YOO-HOO, NINA!

SO, HOW'S THE POOR, LITTLE GIRL DOING?

HELLO, TWINS! THINGS ARE GREAT TODAY! ACTUALLY, MAKE THAT SUPER-MEGA-GREAT!

THAT'S RIGHT CONSIDERING EVERYTHING THAT HAPPENED HERE!

WELL, MY GOODNESS! THE NIGHT BROUGHT A CHANGE IN YOU!

WHAT HAPPENED HERE...? OH! THAT'S NOTHING! NOTHING AT ALL!

YOU THINK? AND DID YOU HAVE TIME TO COPY YOUR LINES IN ADDITION TO THE HOMEWORK ON RAMSES II?

I REALLY STRUGGLED TO FIND ANY SOURCES.

HEY, MISS KLUTZY! WHAT KIND OF GAG WILL YOU PLAY FOR US TODAY?

I--

SHH! DON'T ANSWER! LISTEN!

⸭WHISPER... WHISPER⸭

HUH?— OH YEAH, THAT'S COOL!

WHAT ARE YOU SAYING? WHAT'S COOL?

NO, NO! NOTHING! I HAVE TO GO— WASH MY HANDS BEFORE CLASS!

YOU'RE NOT GOING TO SNUB ME MUCH LONGER!

SHE'S NOBODY. DON'T HURT HER! SHE'S MORE STUPID THAN MEAN!

DON'T WORRY ABOUT IT! SHE JUST NEEDS A LITTLE LESSON!

SO, NINA! YOU CAN'T HEAR WHEN PEOPLE ARE TALKING TO YOU? DO YOU NEED YOUR EARS CLEANED?

IF I WERE YOU, LAURIE, I'D BEHAVE MYSELF.

ORDERS, NOW? WHO DO YOU THINK YOU ARE, SCARECROW? YOUR CLOTHES LOOK A LITTLE DRAB. I'M GOING TO GIVE 'EM A QUICK WASH!

OKAY! THAT'S ENOUGH KIDDING!

HEY! WHAT THE--?

HELP! HELP! NINA! DO SOMETHING!

THAT'S ENOUGH, SYBIL! SHE'S GOT IT!

WHO GETS THE QUICK WASH? HEEHEEHEE!

WELL, WHO WOULD'VE GUESSED--? OUR NINA HAS CHANGED!

I'LL GET YOU, NINA! YOU'LL PAY FOR THAT!

GOOD MORNING, CLASS! BEFORE WE GET STARTED, I'M GOING TO COLLECT YOUR HOMEWORK ON RAMSES II!

WHAT DID YOU DO TO LAURIE? WHERE IS SHE?

I DIDN'T DO ANYTHING! HONEST! HEEHEEHEE!

JENNA! NINA! NO TALKING! YESTERDAY'S EXTRA ASSIGNMENT WASN'T ENOUGH OF A LESSON?

YES, MISS RESSLER, I DID IT! IT'S WITH MY HOMEWORK!

VERY IMPRESSIVE! I PREFER YOU LIKE THIS, NINA!

WELL, LAURIE! YOU'RE LATE! YOU'LL HAVE TO PULL YOURSELF TOGETHER!

YES, MISS RESSLER!

THAT'S YOUR HOMEWORK?! I'M SORRY, BUT YOU'LL HAVE TO REDO IT FOR TOMORROW!

YES, MISS RESSLER!

THANKS TO YOU, LAURIE NO LONGER INTIMIDATES ME! THIS RELATIONSHIP IS REALLY WORKING OUT GREAT!

STICK WITH ME, NINA— THE BEST IS YET TO COME!

WHAT'S THIS--? STINKER BELL IS BACK! THAT PROMISES SOME SPORT!

THE END

38

WATCH OUT FOR PAPERCUTZ™

Welcome to the magical debut of the SYBIL THE BACKPACK FAIRY graphic novel series from Papercutz. By now you probably know who Sybil, Nina, and Pandigole are, but you may not know what a "graphic novel" or "Papercutz" are. Well, I'm Papercutz Editor-in-Chief Jim Salicrup, and I'm here to explain it all to you…

First, "graphic novel" is just a fancy-schmancy term for any kind of comics printed in book form. Secondly, "Papercutz" is the name, dreamed up by Sylvia Nantier, for the publishing company that was created by publisher Terry Nantier and me, and that is dedicated to publishing great graphic novels for all ages. Obviously, we believe that SYBIL THE BACKPACK FAIRY is such a graphic novel, and that's why we're publishing it!

Written by Michel Rodrigue, and illustrated by Antonello Dalena and Manuela Razzi, SYBIL THE BACKPACK FAIRY truly is a wonderful graphic novel for all ages. Each and every page is filled with all sorts of surprises and fun. Obviously, we're just seeing the tip of the iceberg as far as Sybil's world is concerned—so many mysteries are presented here, that even we can't wait for the next SYBIL THE BACKPACK FAIRY #2 "Amanite"!

And if you can't wait until then, in the meantime you may want to pick up another premiere Papercutz graphic novel series, available now at booksellers everywhere: ERNEST & REBECCA #1 "My Best Friend is a Germ." Six and a half year-old Rebecca is sick all the time, her parents are constantly fighting, and her older sister is going through a rebellious phase. Everything changes on the rainy day Rebecca meets a mysterious microbe named Ernest…

If the artwork seems a bit familiar, that's because it's drawn by Antonello Dalena and colored by Cecilia Giumento who both also worked on SYBIL!

Everyone at Papercutz wants to know what you think of SYBIL THE BACPACK FAIRY— so you can send your feedback to me. Just email me at salicrup@papercutz.com or send an actual letter or post card to me at Papercutz, 40 Exchange Place, Suite 1380, New York, NY 10005. Whether you love or hate SYBIL THE BACKPACK FAIRY, let us know! We really want to create the very best graphic novels we possibly can for you, so it really helps us when you let us know what you like or don't like. And be sure to go to www.papercutz.com for a peek at all the other great graphic novels, such as THE SMURFS, GERONIMO STILTON, DISNEY FAIRIES, and so many more, that we publish, as well as for all the latest news on SYBIL THE BACKPACK FAIRY!

Thanks,

Jim

SPECIAL BONUS SECTION!

LIFE WITH SYBIL
the Backpack Fairy

WHAT'S CONVENIENT WITH MY FAIRY IS THAT SHE LIVES IN MY BACKPACK WITH PANDIGOLE, HER PERSONAL ASSISTANT!

...IT'S REALLY THEIR SECOND HOME! THE ONLY DRAWBACK IS PANDIGOLE'S SWEET TOOTH...

NINA! EVERYO HAS TURNED THEIR HOMEWO I'M WAITING F YOURS!

YES, MISS RESSLER! RIGHT AWAY!

..WHICH, SOMETIMES, HAS AWKWARD SIDE-EFFECTS!

AND DO I GRADE YOUR WRITING OR YOUR COLLAGES?

WELL...

÷BURP!÷

MAYBE YOU NEED TO JOIN WEIGHT WATCHERS...?!

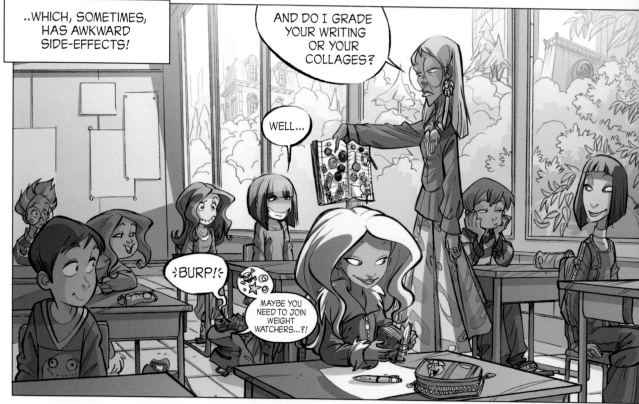

IT'S SO GREAT WHEN SYBIL WHISPERS THE CORRECT ANSWERS TO ME AT SCHOOL!

—AND THAT LEADS TO A RETROACTIVE EFFECT!

MOM! WHAT DOES "RETROACTIVE" MEAN?

IT MEANS THAT YOU APPLY THINGS FROM TODAY TO THOSE OF YESTERDAY OR OF PAST DAYS!

UH...

FOR EXAMPLE, IF I FORGOT YOUR ALLOWANCE LAST WEEK, I'D GIVE IT TO YOU WITH THIS WEEK'S ALLOWANCE!

SOUNDS FAIR TO ME!

BUT THAT DAY, MY FAIRY FELL ASLEEP DEEP INSIDE MY BACKPACK!

YES, NINA? I'M WAITING! WHAT'S THE SOLUTION TO THIS PROBLEM?

WELL— UHH—

UHH— MISS RESSLER! IF YOU ASK ME TOMORROW, I'LL GIVE YOU THE RIGHT ANSWER, AND YOU CAN GIVE ME A RETROACTIVE GRADE FOR TODAY!

?

ALL RIGHT! ZERO FOR THE WRONG ANSWER, PLUS A ZERO FOR BEING A SMART-ALECK!

YEAH, "RETROACTIVE" STINKS AFTER ALL! AND WHAT'S MORE, IT DOUBLES YOUR BAD GRADES!

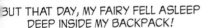

IT'S COOL HAVING A FAIRY AS A FRIEND, ESPECIALLY FOR CHORES!

NINAAA!

YES, MOM!

YOUR BEDROOM LOOKS LIKE A REAL BATTLEFIELD! YOU CAN GO PLAY WHEN IT'S STRAIGHTENED UP!

SIGH!

AND NO GRUMBLING!

SNURF!

DON'T WORRY, NINA! JUST WATCH!

WOW! THAT'S BETTER THAN IN MARY POPPINS!

THE BOOK OR THE MOVIE? DIDN'T READ IT! DIDN'T SEE IT!

DOESN'T MATTER! LET'S GO!

YIPPEE!

AAA—

TCHOOOOO

NINAAA!

EXCEPT WH PANDIGOLE A COLD!

WHAT'S ALSO GOOD ABOUT SYBIL IS THAT I'M THE ONLY ONE WHO CAN SEE HER!

REALLY, NINA, YOU COULD HAVE CHOSEN A MORE FEMININE SPORT!

DANCING **IS** STUPID!*

OKAY, LULU, FOR NINA'S FIRST LESSON, TAKE IT EASY ON HER!

I'M GONNA SMASH THAT SHRIMP! HEHEHEH!

OWWW!

HA!

SOK

I CAN'T WATCH THIS!

ARE YOU OKAY, NINA?

NOT REALLY— LITTLE LULU IS A BRUTE!

LISTEN, I HAVE AN IDEA! *WHISPER!*

YEAH!

SO, SHRIMP? ALREADY GIVING UP?

POW

OUCH!

NAH!

I'VE NEVER SEEN SUCH A PUNCH! YOUR DAUGHTER IS A FUTURE CHAMPION! BUT SHE HAS TO LEARN GOOD SPORTSMANSHIP!

THIS IS ALL MOVING A LITTLE TOO FAST FOR ME!

WE'RE NOT BAD, THE TWO OF US!

*SHE WOULDN'T THINK THAT IF SHE SIGNED UP FOR *DANCE CLASS*—COMING IN 2012 FROM PAPERCUTZ!

WHAT I LOVE ABOUT MY LITTLE FAIRY IS THAT SHE SHOWS ME THINGS NOBODY KNOWS ABOUT!

WHAT'S THE MATTER, NINA?

⁑SIGH!⁑ IT'S RAINING... AND I'M BORED!

OH! LOOK! THERE'S NOTHING SADDER THAN A DEAD, LITTLE BIRD!

CAN YOU BRING HIM BACK TO LIFE, SYBIL?

NO, BUT I'M GOING TO SHOW YOU WHERE HE IS NOW!

MACHINAGAIA!

OOOHHH!

WOW! IS THAT THE BIRDS' PARADISE?

IN A WAY!

WELL, NINA, IS IT THE RAIN THAT'S MAKING YOU SO HAPPY? DID SOMETHING SPECIAL HAPPEN?

YEAH, I GO TO PEEK AT SOMEWHER OVER THE RAINBOW!

WHEN I DO THE COOKING WITH MY LITTLE FAIRY, IT CAN GET VERY CRAZY REAL FAST!

IT'S MOM'S BIRTHDAY TONIGHT! I'M GOING TO MAKE HER A CAKE!

GOOD IDEA! I'M GOING TO HELP YOU!

YUM!

WHICH ONE DO I CRACK FIRST? THIS ONE OR THAT?

MAKE THEM RUN A RACE!

HOW?

ZEEPLA!

WHOA! FUNNY, HEY!

YEAH! GO AHEAD, #8!

THEY'RE OFF! #6 IS GOING TO WIN!

YAHOOOOO!

HEY! WATCH OUT! DON'T LET THEM GET OUT!

DARN! THE DOOR!

TOO LATE!

I'LL BREAK THE SPELL! ZEEEPLA!

NINA, COULD YOU EXPLAIN WHY THESE EGGS ARE IN THE YARD?

UH— I'M PRACTICING FOR EASTER, MOM!

FOR MORE EGG-CITING EGG-VENTURES WITH EGGS, PICK UP *THE SMURFS AND THE EGG* — AVAILABLE AT BOOKSELLERS EVERYWHERE!

WHAT'S SOMETIMES ANNOYING ABOUT MY FRIEND THE FAIRY IS HER ABSENT-MINDEDNESS!

...AND THEY WERE THE LAST THREE MONARCHS OF THE COUNTRY...

⊰WHISPER! WHISPER!⊱

JENNA! NINA! CARE TO SHARE WHAT YOU'RE TALKING ABOUT?

!

UH...

THAT'S NOT VERY INTERESTING! NINA! COME UP HERE INSTEAD AND RECITE TO US THE NAMES OF THE LAST THREE MONARCHS!

⊰SIGH!⊱

WELL?

UH— WELL UH— IT'S... UH---!

⊰WHISPER! WHISPER!⊱

OH, YEAH, THAT'S IT! I KNOW!

EDWARD VIII, GEORGE VI, AND ELIZABETH II!

?

YOUR ANSWER IS CORRECT, NINA, BUT FOR ENGLAND! BUT MY QUESTION CONCERNED FRANCE!

I THOUGHT SO, TOO!

IT'S NOT MY FAULT. I WAS LISTENING TO WHAT JENNA WAS TELLING YOU!

46

WHAT'S GREAT ABOUT MY LITTLE FAIRY ARE HER POWERS FOR PLAYING!

ON THE EVENINGS MY MOM GOES OUT, I BABYSIT MY LITTLE BROTHER. WE HAVE FUN FLYING TO THE CEILING!

OOL! OOL

WHOA! COOL!

IT'S ME, HONEY!

KA-KLAK

OOPSIE! QUICK! COME BACK DOWN!

DID YOU HAVE A GOOD EVENING? AND YOUR BROTHER? IS HE SOUND ASLEEP?

YES, YES!

OOL! OOO!

AAAAH!

LATER...

DON'T WORRY, MA'AM. YOUR CHILD IS IN GOOD HEALTH! YOU'RE NOT USING SKIM MILK?

THE NEXT TIME, TRY NOT TO FORGET HIM UP AT THE CEILING!

YOU SHOULDN'T HURRY ME!

Happy Holidays From PapercutZ

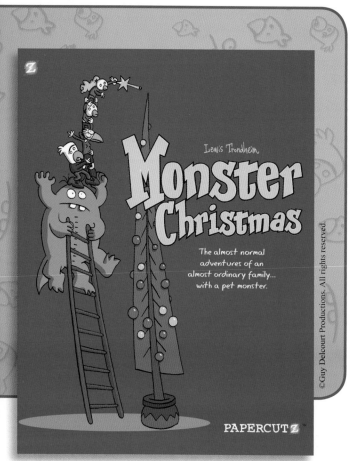

It's Santa Claus versus the Monsters!

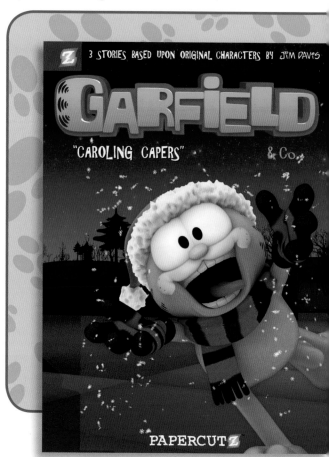

Here are the almost normal adventures of an almost ordinary family… with a pet monster!

Somehow when brother and sister, Peter and Jean, drew a picture of a scary monster, it came alive! Kriss, the monster with with three legs, four arms, and ten mouths, that they created, became the family's pet.

On a Christmas vacation, Kriss, along with Peter, Jean, and their parents, drive to the mountains. But when they witness another monster chasing Santa Claus, they forget all about their vacation plans and do everything they can to save Santa Claus and Christmas!

MONSTER #1 "Monster Mess" is a great new Papercutz series by award-winning cartoonist Lewis Tronheim.

Garfield Sings for his Supper!

Garfield couldn't care less about Christmas until he sees a group of carolers on TV rewarded with tasty holiday treats! Garfield, not known for being especially fast or industrious, is instantly belting out carols to the neighbors in hopes of getting treats for himself! There's just one problem: Garfield can't sing!

GARFIELD & Co #4 "Caroling Capers" features three stories based upon original characters created by Jim Davis, as seen on The Cartoon Network.

Available at Booksellers Everywhere!

Or order from us: please add $4.00 for postage and handling for first book, add $1.00 for each additional book. MONSTER #1 "Monster Christmas" is $9.99 in hardcover only. GARFIELD & Co #4 "Caroling Capers" is $7.99 in hardcover only. Please make check payable to NBM Publishing. Send to: Papercutz 40 Exchange Place, Ste. 1308, New York, NY 10005 * 1-800-886-1223

www.papercutz.com